Levon Shahnur (Shahnazaryan) was born on October 16, 1987. He writes prose and his first collection of stories, *Night of Creation*, was published in 2013. He has received several awards, including the 2015 Russian Speech ("Russkaya Rech") award for Best Prose Piece, with the winning story published in a collection of literature from the Commonwealth of Independent States. His stories are regularly featured in Armenian and international publications. Shahnur's work has been translated into several languages. His novel *Journey: Before Love* was published in 2016. One of his stories, *The Mooneating Newborn*, was developed into a screenplay and movie in 2018. The story also featured in his collection called *The Pain Capturer*, published in 2018. Levon Shahnur is a member of the Union of Writers and the Union of Journalists of the Republic of Armenia.

Levon Shahnur

THE MOONEATING NEWBORN

TRANSLATED BY NAZARETH SEFERIAN

AUSTIN MACAULEY PUBLISHERS™

LONDON • CAMBRIDGE • NEW YORK • SHARJAH

Ordering Information
Quantity sales: Special discounts are available on quantity purchases by corporations, associations, and others. For details, contact the publisher at the address below.

Publisher's Cataloging-in-Publication data
Shahnur, Levon
The Mooneating Newborn

ISBN 9781649793096 (Paperback)
ISBN 9781649793102 (ePub e-book)

Library of Congress Control Number: 2021912810

www.austinmacauley.com/us

First Published (2021)
Austin Macauley Publishers LLC
40 Wall Street, 33rd Floor, Suite 3302
New York, NY 10005
USA

mail-usa@austinmacauley.com
+1 (646) 5125767

I am thankful to my wonderful parents, to my cat, Nico, and to my crow, Markos, for inspiring me.

Oh God, take my soul, but forgive my audacity, for only half of me comes to You...

My family tree had gone missing a long time ago, but I managed to find it recently. The word 'God' appeared on the roots of the tree with dense branches. The trunk said 'Adam,' then 'Noah,' 'Japeth,' and then 'Hayk,' following which the branches bore the names of all my forefathers and ancestors, with one of the extensions reaching my father. I try to add my name to the branch, but my hands are shaking. There is a profound emptiness and an abyss after me because I have no offspring. People like me are called 'unproductive' in my village. When the house is filled with the laughter and giggles of children, their shouting and clacking, and someone suddenly opens the door and pushes them out of the house, the walls of the room seem to narrow and touch each other, the ceiling slowly descends and kisses the floor, objects take on the supernatural and disgusting quality of not breaking, solitude tightens a black tie around my neck and drags me in front of a mirror, where I strike different poses so that I can trick myself into thinking that I am one of those people who smiles, standing with his back bent, surrounded by people who are having interesting conversations. But my house sinks underground and, like someone drowning in the ocean, all I see is the sky, because there will not be another generation after me, which means that I come directly after Adam and, perhaps, God had created me as the progenitor of the world…

My family tree begins with God. When I was small, I asked my grandfather, "How far do the branches go?"

My grandfather thought a bit, picked up the family tree, and told me about the ancestors perching on its branches, counted out their names, and then he said:

"In the end, God is going to come again. His name will always be on the mountain peak. The departing generations are simply a staircase through which the soul ascends to the Lord. There is a powerful thing between the heavens and the earth – life, which threads its way to God."

When I was first placed into my mother's arms, I was like a little piece of moss. An old woman who had seen me struck her hands on the hem of her skirt and said, "Oh dear! The moon has seen this child…"

There's an old tradition that the moon should not cast itself on a newborn until the fortieth day after he or she is born, but it had already seen me. I was born and had spent ten days quietly asleep under its rays, right next to the window. I was the firstborn and ended up being the only child of the family. Terrified by what the old woman had said, my inexperienced mother was trying in vain to draw the curtains, carry me away from the window, and use her eyes to peck at the old woman's face like a bird. But the old woman was shaking her head and saying that it was too late. From that day on, I was dubbed the 'mooneating newborn' in our village. The other kids didn't care, but the mothers looked at me in fear, as if I were a leper. One thing was clear

– day by day, they kept waiting for something to happen to me…

I started to withdraw. Only the elderly men in the village did not recoil when they saw me. Perhaps it was out of respect for my grandfather. I would sit next to them from morning to evening in the village square, on the thick poplar tree log. They would smoke, mumble, shout, and recall times gone by, and they would only remember me when they needed water to be brought from the spring.

I would write poems. I finished school and was walking back to the poplar tree one morning, but there was nobody there. I waited. The door of one of the houses opened. An old man slowly walked up to me and said pensively, "Mooneater, you would know. How's it all going to end?"

A war had broken out.

The elderly men of the village started gathering again, and the women also joined them at the poplar tree. I started to go there again like in the old days. I soon realized that all conversation came to a halt when I appeared, and whispering is unbearable for a moon like me. Their children, my peers, had been taken to fight in the war. They had left me because I was the only child in the family, and my grandfather had died; he was no longer around to press the family tree against my face and hold me back from what I had set my mind on doing…

I had nothing to hide from the world. I was young. My soul was pure. When I was leaving home, my back would feel the taste of emptiness without leaning against anything solid. On my journey out of the village, I acknowledged the increasingly rapid beats of my heart, each rushing ahead of the other for fear of being struck.

My body kept trying to throw itself back into my memories, but I had not lived long enough – my footsteps barely stretched to the mountain slope. The path of life was calling out to me. My closed pores wished to open and smell the gunpowder, to sense the wave of the exploding bomb and cause the back of my neck to break out into goose bumps. All of this lay ahead because I was still young. There was only one exception – my pores would close at any sense of the smell of death, my ears would go deaf, my mind would grow dull, and my poor jaded heart would try to hold on to and calm at least one of my heartbeats. At moments like those, I had to hide life from the world...

"While the moon and the night may have seeped inside me, you are like the sun to me, dear Mama," I told my weeping mother as I was leaving.

They called me the poet on the battlefield. We sat on one of the many hills out there. The enemy sat on the other. For some reason, I had imagined them the way that the elders had described a gargoyle – on all fours, with a tail, and pointy hair spread out untidily.

There was a valley between us and a river hissing through it. Blackened by the everyday fighting, smoke, and dust, we looked longingly at the shimmering water, and the sweat was stinging our bodies. That first agreement remained a mystery, but someone from our platoon had gone down to the other bank of the river and met the enemy who had come down with the same intentions. They had hidden from each other but had not fired. Then they had spoken and agreed that we would go down to the river to bathe in the afternoons on odd-numbered days, and they would go down on even-numbered days, and not a shot would be fired.

I finally saw the enemy – they did not have tails and they splashed their bodies with water just as happily as we did, singing energetically. And then we would do the same. We would go down to the river in single file to splash ourselves under their gaze.

When the time to bathe ended, we would start to fire at each other. Sometimes, I would look at the moon at night and wonder, *Either I have truly been enchanted by the moon and I'm the only one who can see it this way, or all of this becomes a mockery at the clap of nature's hands. After all, don't all the rivers of the world mix their waters with each other?* A smile had come to me from Jordan and had slipped into this river…

I would play in the sand during the day, and by night, I would lie on my back and gather the moon in the palm of my hand, trying to squeeze it slightly so that I could hear its screech. In the fall, the leaves rustled under my feet and looked upwards like orphans, to the branches that bore them…

Perhaps I really was a poet. I felt all kinds of strange feelings awaken within me, and I was making small cradles of wood, especially during shelling, chaotic sounds flooded inside me – children screaming and crying as if a whole tribe had gathered in my soul and was running from wall to wall in fear, rocking the cradles as they went.

In my dreams, the dull light from the moon fell upon everyone – the door and windows were fully open and I could see the sparkling particles of light. My mother would run and shut this door, clamp that window, and draw the curtains that would rip immediately, and the moonlight would once again fall on the cradles…

"Why are you just standing there?" she would shout at me. "They're going to die…"

The people fighting against me also had family trees, and I fired ten or twenty rounds the way a cross-eyed soldier would… on a whole tribe. After the battles, the fields would start moaning; someone was striking down dozens and would then start to sweep them away. Someone would use one leg to take flight. The other would use an arm. Yet another would lie on his back with his legs shaking in the air, while the rest, lying immobile, would slowly shrink and recoil into a small pit.

People were dying. Gagik's name meant 'mountain peak.' Babken was named as the youngest son of his father, Khoren, who had been named after the sun. Nature was dying both on our hilltop and on the one opposite.

One of the wounded boys in our platoon asked me to write a letter to his lover that would make her miss him even more…

I wrote it.

When I was reading it out, the boys sitting around grew emotional, and then they all replaced the name of the girl with those of their girlfriends and sent the letters home. There was a Russian-speaking boy in our platoon. He had lived in Moscow and could not write in Armenian. We translated it into Russian so that he could send it home, but he never made it. He died during one of the battles, and we could not find his copy of the letter.

The months went by. Sometimes we'd retreat. Sometimes we'd advance, but we almost always remained on those two hilltops. It was like standing on ice – we wanted to hold on to one another, but we would slip and end up falling upon one another. Despite all this, we kept bathing in the river.

We would discover copies of my letter in the pockets of the enemy soldiers – either written in Russian or translated into their own language. Only the names of their lovers were changed. The rest was the same on our side, and it was the same on theirs. The letter was the river where all of us would be sprinkled with one love. That same letter is read out throughout the world. Only the names are changed, just like life.

I woke up in a military hospital.

"Well? How are you doing?" the man on the cot next to me asked.

I slipped my hands beneath the sheet. It was empty, a profound pit – I was a treasure, and death had dug deep on all four sides to get to me.

"There would be no footprints on my path… my poetry. My heart would run in front of a train with two ridiculous crutches…"

I closed my eyes because I yearned for the moon…

The man next to me groaned:

"What can I say… We need to forget everything we know…"

That evening seemed peaceful to me. Those few words rang true – *we need to forget everything we know*. This is the last struggle of a dying man.

I imagined the look in the eyes of my lover when she spotted something interesting and turned her face away from me. I was looking at her eyes, which were crooked; they shone. Oh God! They glittered but not for me…

I am starting to forget.

I forget my parents, my brothers, my sisters, the people I love, my friends, all the homeless dogs in the world, and the beggars who knock on my door. I forget the seasons, the dates on the calendar, the minutes, and the times when I admired the body of a beautiful woman as a map of the world… I even love your aging wrinkles so that I can later call out, "Mary, Mary, Mother of God…"

My legs, my hands, and my body – I forget to look at all of you. I lean against a tree like a drunkard when I leave home, and I fall to the ground, crawling. I chew on my daily bread with the vacant stare of a laborer who has leaned against the cold wall he has built…

I need to forget everything. I'm young. My mind is being woven like a thread fallen in a carpet. How can I forget, old man? "Forget!"

I forget the white walls, the moribund color of the hospital. I forget my mother's tears as she tries to embrace my handicapped body and we both fall to the ground. I forget her despairing gulps and the curses she directs at those who make war. I look out the window to see couples kissing and I forget the water on my lips. My dog tugs at the hollow legs of my trousers so that we can go and run around like we used to. I forget…

Oh Lord, if the moon that I ate was to blame for all this, then why could I not forget its yellow light? If a scissors has cut off the branch on which I was supposed to stand with a loved one and many sons and daughters, why did you leave the path to reach you unfinished?

The family tree hanging on the wall is silent. Had I forgotten the story of one of my ancestors who was finding himself unable to have a son and then cut off the apricot tree in his orchard and squatted on the stump for days, spreading out his hands and holding his fingers wide open, becoming a tree himself? People were saying that he had lost his mind, but he was praying that his family tree would not dry up, and he ended up having a son – my grandfather. My tie of solitude once again attaches itself to me and drags me in front of the mirror...

I would then lie down in my bed. They will cover the mirrors with sheets and draw the curtains shut. The mewing cats and howling dogs will gather next to the moon, but they will drive these animals away from me. They won't light any candles above my head because I am the moon-eating man. People will sit at the head of my bed and mourn because they will see that I truly was the moon. I was also the progenitor of the entire world in my colors of yellow and white.

But the moon is not a source of light; it reflects the light from the sun. My mother, the sun, will come, sit next to my faded body, and speak:

"If only warmth, the air, light, day and night, rivers and lakes, birds and rocks, waves and the lights that sparkle above them, and colonies of ants in the millions could be kneaded like bread, if only people would make balls of this dough, mash it with hands and bake peace with love every day... perhaps then there would be no time for war, and you would be able to have an heir, my son. Then our family tree would reach up to God."

Inside the 女 character

… She said we live in a round world where there is a larger language. We need to restrain it, so that we can learn to talk to each other and be together.

I woke up and opened my eyes, and there was the same silence of breathing, the calm in which one can hear ants going about their work. I swung my legs off the bed and lowered them to the floor, put my hands on my knees and stood up, walked to the kitchen, and turned on the light while it was still dawn. My pathological desire to speak had numbed. I searched for the coffeepot and my ears were soon seeking words. Did anyone have the desire to speak at all? Where was she?

I distilled my tongue and barely managed to reach her with the last remaining word. I had been given a limited quantity, a small amount, to live and also 'love.' One could not love in the city because to love would mean to speak a lot, and people therefore avoided wasting their vocabulary in this way so that they did not die early; they saved them for a rainy day so that they could seek a favor here or there when it came to their careers and so on. I fell in love and began to waste the words I had been allotted. When the time came to build a home and when the moment arrived to seek a job, I had no words left but everything was buzzing around me. My family, friends, and acquaintances took out the words that they had tucked aside and got to work.

I used three words today – 'new computer program.' My parents are convinced that I'm no longer wasting my words but, from this day on, I'm using a recorder and saying things – which means I have suicidal tendencies – because people are born with a limited vocabulary in our times. I don't know the exact quantity of words I've been allocated. I assume it's not a big number, because three days ago, a drunk person spoke and then died right before my eyes. People tried to cover his mouth with handkerchiefs, but he was drunk and his words just flooded out, which was a certain path to death… And so, the first day I thought something out loud, a chair fell over in the corner of the pub, and the guy sitting on it kept staring upwards with a smirk, but nobody tried to help him up, not even me. It could damage my wellbeing. Perhaps he would say something that would trigger my conscience – if such a thing exists – and extract a word out of me. Many people do that nowadays – one word, one day… Such people are increasing in number these days. They are against the system, but they seek revenge from those similar to them, and the fallen man said, "Hi everyone, hello lights, hello chairs, glasses, bottles…" And he kept going. The others on the scene tried to gag his mouth shut because life was flowing out of it, like the blood from the arteries of an animal that had been cut, but he kept pulling those hands away and shouting, "I'm going to finish my word stock today…" I looked at the demented man and the ice cube growing warm in the whiskey. The man was dying. The ice was melting. I needed to make a bet on which would end sooner, but who could I bet against if it meant I had to use words? Explaining the point of the bet would take at least twenty days off my life, and the other person would not help by asking questions. He would not say a single word to make things easier for me, which was why I decided to bet against myself in my mind, and this was not the first time I did this. Every ten minutes, the sound of an instrument made of molded metal could be heard, because real music would only spur thoughts, and that is rife with the threat of speaking. There was a girl sitting two chairs away. A couple that separated from that wave of confusion walked up to her and rolled her over, laughing and roaring. They were probably a drunken married couple. Perhaps they had not spoken for days so that they could come here today, drink – after waiting for four years, sleeping pressed up against each other, and looking into each other's eyes – and speak the words they had waited so long to say after all kinds of interesting, adventurous preparations, delivering one or two words to each other, and finding relief. They came and rolled over this girl. I smashed my glass to the floor and shouted, "Enough!" Everyone there looked at me in shock, even the drunk man who had been lifted to his feet with his mouth gagged. The modern human was not supposed to waste his words, especially for strangers. He could stub someone's toe and not say sorry, opting instead to simply press the recorder's 'forgive me' button. The girl got up from the floor, straightened her chair without noticing me, and then sat down again. I walked up to her, took her by the arm, and we left the pub.

***

… There's a glass of whiskey in front of me. I look through it at my palms, which are pressed up against the glass like snails. There was a shout from the corner bench in the pub. I can't recall what they said. Fresh words are such a rarity that our ears have been plugged shut, making words coming from the throat very difficult to catch. The man spoke and was drunk. The people there had stared at him in shock.

I tell her this story again. She cries and puts her head to my chest, pressing her palms to my mouth so that I would not speak. I repeat the words that have been spoken in her presence as well. I could have recorded the words spoken by others and played them back to her without spending any from my own stock, but I repeat it all in my voice because I'm tired of restraining myself by hiding my thoughts. Meanwhile, she keeps pressing the 'quiet' button on her recorder – "Quiet! Quiet!" …

I shut up, swaying and leaning on her. Then I find my own recorder in my pocket and press the 'that's all' button. I swipe through the templates on the screen and press 'calm down.' I hug her and look over her shoulder as I go through the menu options to find something pleasant to say but I can't. My eyes get blurry. She pulls back and puts a finger to her nose, meaning 'be quiet and wait,' and she presses the template we like on her screen – "Words will run out. Recorders will break down, but our love will never dry up."

She says that we can take sign-language courses meant for the deaf and mute, but I'm against the idea. Hand movements change the nature of my thoughts, and each word tries to find a finger of its own, or its own movement, and it emerges completely changed. I consider this to be a sign of weakness. In the past, poets would sing out their whole word stock and die. They ran out of vocabulary at a young age and lay down in ecstasy in their beds, because they were not afraid and had not hidden their words so that they could nurse themselves to longevity like us. I've always thought that anyone who dies young is a genius.

Words considered unnecessary are no longer used these days, and the names of the days, weeks, months, and years remain unspoken. The weather of the day is left without description. No one calls out to anyone's window in the mornings, and the first snow of the season does not cause any delight. Salespeople take care to make sure that nobody has to waste any words in their hypermarkets – you pick up the list at the entrance that suits you best, and you walk to do your shopping. It could be a list of ingredients for lunch or dinner, a meal plan for a diet or a vegetarian, and the districts in the poorer parts of town use pages torn out of books – sections cut out of Russian novels, for example – where you can find delicious pies, jam, and vodka.

Distil the tongue. Dilute it to the extent that only one or two words are left, perhaps even the ones from different ends of the same sentence, joined together without a connection. To me, you are a voice living far away. Get rid of the 'to me,' the 'you,' the 'are,' a voice living far away. This is where it becomes torturous to choose among these words. Can we combine the 'voice' with the 'far away' or perhaps we can fuse the 'living' with the 'voice' …

And there are thus voices that live far away (in abandoned houses where the winds leave the sound of pain, the screeches of the night which weave presumed stories in one's mind, the growling of a dog, and the sounds of pebbles under one's feet …) and I hear them but not waste them. Water – I drink water incessantly so that I don't speak and can tell her let's go somewhere far away, where afar is a relative thing, far away from our previous spot, to be in the distance we know and think once again about it. Take me to the remote places where we can allocate some time during the day to thinking, and we will blend our words together like a dying flame so that they can smolder and bring forth new ones such that we don't die. And then we'll drink, we'll make merriment, we'll go mad, and we'll take turns drawing in the air from the balcony or a door left ajar. We'll draw it in and blow it out in the room. We'll pitch a tent together in that distant place and submit ourselves to the pressure of the night sky such that the stars keep falling towards our heads and come so close that we cannot move because the night sky tends to drop down and hang close over us. I'm thinking about you today with the serenity of an old man. This is a stronger yearning that an excited one, and I bring it closer to you with the curses of an old woman.

People carry recorders with various cliché phrases on them. They swipe through the sentences to find the ones they want and tap on the screen. Pronunciation is replaced by recordings. If it is a man, he can choose a suitable voice and press: *'I'll be at home in the evening'* or *'Turn off the light.'* There are special recorders on sale for children, with answers to the presumed questions that they have not yet asked – No. 1: *'clouds.'* Tap that button and the recorder will say, "The layer of air around the planet, consisting of a mixture of gases."

There are families that hire young people as temporary workers and enjoy real, fresh words. They either give them their own writing to read or pick the lines of an old poet's verses. Thus, there are fewer recorders in rich families. These people are surrounded by voices coming from the throat.

Lately, I get drunk and talk all kinds of nonsense, enough to exhaust my stock – I've already lost count of my word expense – which I plan to replace with the intention to know the moment of my death. She grows angry at my attempts at suicide and threatens me with starting to work again as a contracted voice for others. This shuts me up because I cannot imagine any other misfortune like it. Their work in these luxurious mansions is undignified and they are paid peanuts. She would stand absently next to the woman who had hired her and repeat the words coming out of a recorder. She would sometimes go completely blank, and the lady would nudge her, pressing the 'stupid' icon on the recorder and having a laugh with her rich girlfriends. I was forced to read a few scribbles by a book-loving official to make some money and pay off her owners so that I could bring her back home.

The voice coming from the devices is hateful to me. "I understand," is said by the voice of a criminal who has been given a more lenient imprisonment or perhaps a more nuanced death sentence in exchange for reading and recording those words, which are then sold. Any new recording is advertised in a billion ways. There are recorders that have children's voices. They're reading fairytales. Some of them even have lisps, and these are bought by young families who switch them on for their children in the evenings.

The person who says 'I love you' on my recorder is a miserable being – no matter how much they have tried to adjust it and give his vocal chords a blissful touch, I can still sense the nausea felt by the person. Perhaps he is a murderer who was sentenced to death after he was made to speak and be recorded.

The templates that have been expressed with real love are expensive. Couples like us can't afford to use them. There are rich families who hire poets or readers at expensive rates for their parties. They perform folk songs with crisp voices.

***

She spills the library books on the floor because I've come home drunk again, and my mouth just won't shut up. Our neighbors no longer rush to her aid. I curse and kick them so they are afraid that they will run out of patience and they will be forced to say something bad to me in return. They cherish each day that's left to them and think uninterruptedly so as not to make a mistake and let a word slip out. I watch her desperate movements while she tries to rescue me. She finds and brings a book, shaking as she opens the first page and pushes it in my face. It says, "There were hermits in the past who withdrew to the deserts and worshipped the thought of silence." I laugh at her naivety and at her desperate attempts to keep me silent. I throw the book aside and declare:

"Silence finds its spot around us, and especially within us, even without any worship. We have become silence, and here you are suggesting that we worship it... I don't need silence. I find it disgusting to speak through templates. Whenever I notice something beautiful, I'm forced to seek the right template to tell you about it, to recount something to you, to talk to you, while the words I am often offered have nothing in common with my thoughts... I need my own voice. I live within my own head. I've talked to you there so many times that there are clones of us in my head. They love each other. They ask questions to the people they meet. They come up with answers. They live in the old world where there were no recorders, and words were not counted. They've enumerated them now and allocated a certain stock to us. They put devices inside us when we're born that keep track of our word usage so that they can stop our hearts the moment we run out of stock. I can't go on like this... After all, the poets have always sung for me. It is them that I believe."

She presses her recorder (for a female voice that makes me vomit on the walls). A slutty voice says, "We're together. That's all that matters." I jump to her side. She tries to hide her recorder, but I grab it and smash it against the wall and stomp on it. She's mute now. I take out my recorder. She is hanging by my arms because we will end up being silent for months – until we can save enough money to buy a new one, we will be devoured by silence. I push her aside and slam my recorder to the floor, obliterating it. I embrace her and lift her from the ground. "Calm down," I tell her. "All I'm doing is listening to the voices." I drop our clothes to the floor, open our suitcases, and place them on the bed, and she is by my side. She is under my arm. I take her to the map and put my finger on a desert. She agrees.

We turn to the suitcases. There is an older recorder model hanging from my suitcase. She slowly walks up to it and I am disheartened. I do not have the strength to stop her. She picks it up and, without looking in my eyes, switches it on from the beginning. I woke up and opened my eyes, and there was the same silence of breathing...

She listens to my words for an hour and a half, where only the clones in my head speak, travel, and talk about various remarkable sights...

She weeps and I whisper with my head hung low:

"Because I'm a writer, I can't help but express my thoughts – what I see and what I hear. I can't wait any longer. I've been talking for a long time, even back at my parents' place. Silence transforms itself when it comes to me... I am a man of the head. I've already made a copy of you and everything else around me. They're all in my head, while you have been completely consumed by thought and it has defeated you..."

She presses her lips together. Her hands wrap around her body like moss and she coils it. She walks out the door and I get a sideways view of her heels disappearing out of view, and it doesn't fit in my head, and it makes me miss her.

Without saying a word, she goes back to her old job so that she can exhaust her words.

I submerge into my own head, where I no longer feel like talking... to the woman without the heels.

Nova[1]

I am at that age now when all I hear around me is the news of yet another relative or family member who has passed away. It seems unlikely, but I had not heard the news of anyone dying before this. Now I get bad news every day; I am at the age of the revelation of death. This is where it is trying to defeat me.

"Like a scorpion condemned into a circle of fire, I have stung myself with thoughts about death."

Evelina hears me but mocks me, saying that the watermelon vendor had taught her how to distinguish the rich red content of watermelons hidden beneath their skins – if the sound came from the outside, then it was unripe. If the insides were sonorous, it was ready. She says that if death always comes in red, then she would be able to figure it out. She puts her ear to my stomach and taps on various parts of it and then decides that death has not yet ripened because the sound had come from the outside.

---

[1] In astronomy, a "nova" is a star that demonstrates an unusual increase in luminosity, shining intensely for several days, after which it returns to its former level of luminosity.

We heard about an old lady named Soné and found her in a distant settlement. In Soné's case, she did know how to recognize death and to grab it before it struck unexpectedly. She was a well-known death seer in those villages. When people noticed an unusual change in the appearance of someone they knew. They would call her so that she could take a look and tell them her opinion. If death had already settled in, she would tell them how many days were left. If the suspicions were unfounded, she would calm the family down and tell them that there was no danger. The people who called her over would give her a photograph of the person or point him out from a distance and she would observe secretly from afar, such that the person would not know. After all, everyone knew her, and it is no pleasant thing to discover that the death seer is staring at your face.

"Rarely, one can bear the presence of death for a long time," she said, referring to the coffin-maker of their village, who had been hearing everyone say how young and handsome he was getting over the past two years and had managed to live with death even after Soné had revealed the truth to him.

My mother would laugh when she recalled how I had been born. "I was doing some ironing. The only other person at home was Mané, your cousin on your paternal aunt's side. She died just a few days after that. When my labor pains began, Mané told me to drop that iron, but I continued to go over your father's shirts with even closer attention to detail. Your father had left for work and we had just moved to an unfamiliar part of town. I had spread out the sleeves of his shirt and was eliminating the wrinkles in them so that he would embrace me."

I asked Soné – during my birth, there was someone in the room who was close to death, a young woman. I've heard that this is a bad sign. Am I going to die young or is this just meaningless superstition?

She did not respond, but she mentioned some of the signs that death is close – the nose gets sharper, the face grows indescribably beautiful if the person is ill. Then he or she grows more active and the mood improves.

She said they hated me at home when we were young girls. I saw my sister one morning and was left openmouthed. She had grown so pretty. Her face was shining, and she was giggling, constantly joking and prancing about. She was happy. She was going to be engaged soon to a boy she loved, but I saw an unusual luminosity in her. I told my mother that my sister had grown extremely beautiful that day. My mother cried – my parents knew about by unusual gift. My father locked me up in the cellar that day and said, "I don't want to hear you say anything ever again…" My sister did not find out, but she had sensed something; when my mother started feeding her with honey, combing her hair and kissing her more frequently, she no longer had any doubt. I kept avoiding her, but she chased me constantly so that she could ask me again – is something bad going to happen? I would say, "No, I don't know what you're talking about. Leave me alone." We buried her two weeks later. Death can also be infectious. It can transmit from one person to the other, like all other kinds of pain, and my mother went to great lengths to take the curse upon herself.

When we left her place, Soné gave us some honey and gifted us a comb. She caressed Evelina's hair and, referring to me, she said, "Let him comb your hair sometimes. It's a sign of love." Evelina winked at me, messed up her hair, and gave me the comb. Then she laughed and said, "It'll be all tangled up by the time we get to town. Then you can comb it."

I accept and carry death with me everywhere so that I can study it closely.

The dead or dying that I had met briefly would leave only little details behind, mostly everyday actions, like how the water would flow out of the corners of their mouths when they took a drink or how the contents would drip from the bottom of their cup onto their forehead. Some of the people from the same generation recall these things and even they remember them only once in their lives. I would see many of them often in dreams and notice how only that one action, that one gesture, remained – a slight twitch of bending down or straightening up. That's all.

Sometimes, I cling to Evelina like a madman so that she is careful and stays far from the traps laid by death, because everyone I know says that she's very pretty. She shaves off half of her hair in such a way that the other half falls across and covers the bald patch. "This is to ward off death," she says. I like it; what matters is that it calms me down, and I can focus once again on myself.

She says, "One day, I'm going to stare at one of your lively eyes for hours and talk to them... play with them. You won't know it, but they will see, laugh, and have fun. You will feel that your eyes are rolling me about, picking me up, balancing me, turning me upside down, and giggling like a child. You won't understand why your eyes are so happy and I won't tell you. It will be my little secret."

I take a picture of my face every day and stare into the mirror the next day, with the photo from the previous day in my hand, trying to spot any obvious differences so that I can tie up any loose ends.

With the photo from yesterday in my hand, I rush to see Evelina so that we can go from village to village and listen to the elders speak; their heads have squeezed out some valuable words from life. They are like wet bodies – you can't see anything while they're still in the sea but as they age, they step ashore and the large number of drops on them becomes visible.

She turns her head in the distance as if to say, "See?" As long as this bald patch remains, we have no need to fear death. I come closer – her small nose, her cheeks, her face, her lips, her eyes... She has grown strangely beautiful. Stunned, I look around and see Soné sitting on a park bench close by, watching her from behind a crumpled newspaper. I am curious to know who has told her.

I grab Evelina's head and mess up her hair, smudge her lipstick on her face, and bite her cheek, hurting her; I try to make her ugly to drive death away. I even run my fingers across the knife in my pocket with the intention of making small scratches on her face and ruining it. Her eyes well up and, upset, she tears herself away from me and runs away.

I no longer look at Soné. I have to catch up with Evelina, feed her some honey, and comb her hair so that I can drive death out of her body and into mine.

The Writer's Legs

If you see a stork in flight, the future holds a long journey ahead for you.

The doctor said, "Try to avoid any active movement with your leg; don't use it." My legs' ability to walk must be suppressed. If I set them down on the ground, they'll run, which is why I keep the broken one slightly elevated, and I use a walking stick to hop around when I need to move. I keep it reined in; walking and running away is the only thing it knows how to do. The foot I keep away from the ground twists to the left and right, confused, while I recall the joint attempt the two of them had made to kill me, so I press and release the fracture when the doctor isn't looking so that it wouldn't heal.

My legs have stretched out and want to move from one place to the other to change the world. They take steps with no regard for my own will. Like a pair of noblemen, they stretch themselves upward and without changing the distance between them, they dispassionately settle on the ground. My arms imitate their movements in the air, as if to pretend that they are taking part in my body's mobility, but they know in reality that the machine is moved by the legs.

They are disconnected from the path, and they cannot do anything except to form a fist and then open up, because they lost the ability to fly a long time ago.

My whole body submits to the authority of my legs; I am a creature of my plane, crawling on the floor, and my pleasure at going up and down is short-lived because my legs have reached the floor and they are once again striving to move my body. There is no longer any strength left to resist. I sometimes manage to modify my course to an insignificant extent, to change my position, but nevertheless, encouraged by firmness, my legs end up victorious.

My father says, "Don't go to a psychologist. I'll build you a tree house and you can live there for a while and dangle your legs below so that they swing in the emptiness without a firm surface on which to lean. Time will go by and, as they suffer, they will admit defeat and calm down."

And that is what we do. I spend several days sitting or lying on planks in the tree. My father climbs up and carries me down when nature calls. This touches me. "Father, I don't have a disability. How can I keep doing this? I don't understand…"

"It'll be over soon if you don't let yourself think about leaving. There's a certain age, a mental state, when you can no longer swallow what you see. It sticks permanently to your eyes. And you start to stare blankly, and people try to read what's in your eyes but they can't. They say, 'You're staring blankly. That means someone is on his way here.' But you're sure that your mind has already dressed up and, without looking in the mirror to make sure it's chosen the right words, is ready to leave. When you dangle your legs in the air for long enough, they begin to twitch with discomfort. As soon as you put them on the ground, they'll run."

Sometimes I think that they've recovered. I test them with my father; I slowly put my feet on the ground. My father is next to me, grabbing my shoulder. A few steps later, they bask in the taste of the soil and shamelessly take control. My father grabs me and carries me back up the tree.

I confess to my father that I have seen a stork in flight. He mutters, "You should have told me sooner." He leaves me in the tree house and goes to find the person who sees off travelers. At noon, he's standing with a hunchbacked old man at the foot of the tree. The person who sees off travelers did not have a back. Instead, a mass of flesh seemed to have fused into its place. It was like the secrets of many paths had grown into that part of his body. I had heard that he did not remember when his hunchbacked life had begun, but he now stooped so low that he could only see people's legs and, if he pushed the limits of his curved back, then perhaps their waist. But there was the whole ground before him – the world of land.

There were pebbles and ants down there and, in his own words, this land of below became dear to him, while the movements above grew alien…

He was a unique book, with trials, adventures, carriages, ships, and ponies. When you talked to him, you felt like setting off on a journey, and the fame of this hunchbacked person spread from one village to the other. As soon as someone felt restless, or the need awakened to go somewhere far away, he or she would come to the person who sees off travelers to find out how to suppress this desire. And if there was no way to put an end to it, at least listening to his advice helped them prepare better so that the expected journey would pass without peril.

The person who sees off travelers says that the course is ever-flowing. "Even if you stay where you are, it will reach you and pave its path through you. But it stands still when there is a pause. The pauses make up the holes in the ground that swallow movement, and the others… In your case, it is your father, who has cut you off from the ground."

When you are on your journey, believe that in the places you have left behind and where everyone you know is dead, never look back. If you look back, all the trees and rocks you left behind will appear before you and you will end up in the planet's rotation.

Remember tomorrow, dive in, and recall it in detail because man holds the coming day within him as well. All he needs to do is find it and open it. *If you find the key to the coming day, your present time is safe from harm…*

Don't believe what the weather forecast says. Ask any random old men you meet in the villages – will it rain today or is it going to be sunny? They will give the natural answer, the one that suits your journey.

"It's windy. There will be rain."

"The sun is prickly. It's going to rain."

"The wind is clearing the streets for snow."

"It's going to pour buckets of rain. The angels have been drinking all morning and, since there are no walls or corners in heaven, they will urinate down upon us."

The person who sees off travelers is drinking some tea and tastes an apple from my tree house. He has reached the distant settlements and is issuing warnings – even if the person there is an iron bridge, don't walk over him. This means that it is not a place to be trusted...

My father and the person who sees off travelers are getting ready to go to town to buy groceries. I ask for cigarettes and any book they can find. The person who sees off travelers forbids the book because those are the things that infect people with wanderlust. Before leaving, my father issues orders from below the tree. "Don't you dare stand on the ground and do something foolish. Don't be ashamed of the state you're in. It's common for writers to be overcome with the urge to travel."

The creak of the closing gate can be heard as he leaves. This important sound has also been picked up by my legs as if they are another person, and they have decided to walk. I submit myself to my legs at the head of the tree ladder, to their animal pleasure, their robotic army march. Proud and taut, they smell the soil and freeze for a moment, dig in a bit, and then twitch in the hole they have dug and move forward...

I don't know how long I go with them, but the village is now on the other side of the mountain. My volition remains alive only in my eyes. With a tree sawn off, only an injured stump remaining, an uneven and sharp-toothed field, I'm in the depths of someone's maw, the horned mountains, screeching birds, howling dogs, bleating lambs, clouds swelling with gray color, and the ground growing dark in patches. My knees, completely disconnected from me, suck my blood, using some of it for their task of folding and unfolding and sending the rest to the capillaries in my soles, which touch the ground, get infected, and then carry this contagion back to my heart...

Like overflowing waters that cannot be brought back, I was the same; I had risen above my banks and could not be contained.

Except for my eyes, all the other parts of my body succumb to those ground-loving beings. Even my arms start to row and help them. As the only advantage I hold, I cast my gaze into the distance and call for help, but there is no response. Even if I am to meet someone, they would not consider it prudent to fulfill my request and break my legs or carry me home. I would soon be afflicted with the curse of: "May your eyes be sewn shut!" The sun pours over the cliffs like a freshly cracked egg. The wind extracts mosaic pebbles from their burrows and rolls them along. The lip-smacking 'oohs' and 'ahs' of dry tongues can be heard from the abyss, my mental efforts to escape from 'when.' I climb up onto a plain. A space that was once swallowed by recesses, coming across cliffs and twisting, presses against the hills, suddenly breaking free and flying towards me. The more I strained my eyes on the space before me, the more I could not catch up with it. It is now free and, evading me, stretches into the unknown horizon.

I hang my head as I look at the sinister legs, which smile as they quicken their pace towards the edge of the cliff… ("Resist!"). I try to follow the advice of the person who sees off travelers, and to recall the coming day, certain assumptions begin to take shape, but the impassable spaces that could slow my course as pauses and my father's readiness have all been left behind. (*"Don't look back!"*) *I need the details of the day that is to come.*

My Defeat

There are three sorts of people: those who are alive, those who are dead, and those who are at sea.

Aristotle

I was defeated today. This is a fact, but a question remains: by whom or what? I feel a sense of defeat, but I cannot find its source. There are people that rebel and are defeated but may or may not accept this fact. Armies are defeated by armies and athletes by athletes. But it is different in my case – I fully realize that something is kneeling inside me, but I nonetheless, fail to understand who or what prompted this feeling of having a sword to my neck, forcing me to think about defeat…

"Defeat is followed by depression," say those that have gone down the path of defeat.

There is probably a reason behind every person, but I think about it and cannot find it. Perhaps I lost to God when he created me and then scornfully concealed himself so that I would end up playing hide-and-seek with him and we would end up screaming with joy when I found him? Perhaps it was to Nietzsche's reasonable madness, which was also a consequence of defeat because he thought of victory banners but submitted to the warm delusions of the defeated, or perhaps to Don Quixote, who was in fact Christ at an older age and in his second coming, while people are still kneeling in anticipation of that second appearance, although it took place ages ago.

She calls and excitedly tells me about her business trip and the fascinating customs that the Japanese practice. I say, "I feel like I'm facing defeat…" She pauses for a long time and then sighs deeply and her voice rings out shrilly, "Never admit defeat. Only the weak are defeated. You must always be victorious. Find this part of yourself. Talk to you later."

It's been about two minutes. The phone is still at my ear, even though the call has ended, and I'm staring at a bare-necked nail in the wall. In my childhood, my father had hung the Lord of Defeat on the wall and told me, "As soon as you feel like you're going weak, stand in front of this and say, 'Lord, I think I am facing defeat,' and He will understand you."

I finally separated myself from the phone. She was also one of those that considered people like me to be trash.

My own defeat took place on a shadowy day in the fall. The vision of death appeared so lonely that I had the desire to be the victim of a great catastrophe and ascend to the sky with a large group of people. (In their heart of hearts, everyone wants to die at the same time as everyone else.) And perhaps it was the fear that I felt lost everywhere – even when I had my address written in my palm, I would end up on a different street and completely lose my head – which led me to think that I would not find the way up when I died…

I think one of the signs is that 'sooner or later' is a constant state with me – the future suddenly happens, with every minute detail, and the signs of defeat appear. This is just one possible version...

I am defeated and I start to write. Doing this, I elicit the pleasant feelings of the past when people would wake up, rush to the edge of the river, and tell the flowing water the dreams they had the previous night and then return home with a sense of relief. As the elders say, narrate your dreams to flowing water, and your worries will be carried far from you with the current.

What I'm wondering is who reads those dreams at the other end of the river? Perhaps the river flows past a settlement that leads a different kind of life where people walk toward the same water at dawn and hear or read the dreams that the water has brought with it. It might not matter if they are good dreams or bad. Perhaps those inhabitants have long lost the ability to dream and miss it.

The narrator and listener should often switch places – if one person loses the ability to dream, the other can tell him or her their dreams and remind them so that defeat does not settle deep into the chest of the dreamless person.

I had lost the ability to dream for a long time. Nobody shared their dreams with me, and I was defeated. Nothing serious there – I had simply reached an age where my life had split similar to how a watermelon spreads out in different directions when someone drops it. I begin to notice time in its three distinct pieces, and there is a clear border between the past and what is yet to come.

The lord of the perpendicular waits for my final choice. I have to say that he does that with patience, in silence, like

41

someone standing above you and staring at your scalp, unblinking, and you feel the presence of that gaze, but you have no way of providing the same attention in return.

So I will move back from the border to the depth of memories where people differ from their current image (Even though their names are the same, their gait and gestures are unchanged. They have an identical nose and mouth.) but they are decidedly different in my memories of them. I prefer the closeness we felt in the repetitions of our past, even though I realize that, in this way, I am estranging myself from them in the present. This is a dangerous thing to do, since reliving each memory takes you further on the path of solitude.

I am on a path to another defeat. The horizon is in front of me, where the sky and the ground are locked in a kiss. I want to approach that kiss, but the closer I get, the more their lips open and separate from each other.

This is a small tour of emptiness. I've heard that one can be subjected to an honorable defeat, which is why I chose the creative world of work, because it is the only place (a rocky mountain summit) where I can create and wage my righteous battle with no enemies or rivals.

Salt is not rubbed into the wounds of the defeat you suffer here. This is why I withdrew into the world of words.

I recently started reading a book about ancient Armenian beliefs and I came across the following tradition. A 'writer' was considered to be an angel that goes from building to building, looking into houses where there is an elderly person or someone confined to bed by infirmity, noting down their names and passing them on to the sky so that they can be remembered and called to the heavens. Of course, I am not an angel, and my cigarettes have long burned by delicate wings. Nevertheless, I enjoy this title. I think that in the near future, I will establish myself in this forgotten position. I will go from village to village, finding the people that have stories or secrets hidden away in their minds. I will find the elderly people that still have real words concealed beneath their noses. They have hidden those words away for years without telling them to anyone so that they can pass them on to a writer. And I, too, will finally have a profession, and people will understand that writing is not like a pastime or morning exercises for the torso. The 'angel writer' elicits everyone's stories because it is these very secrets that cause earthquakes and volcanic eruptions after they are buried in the ground. It is because their rightful place is in speech, or rather in writing, and on the path to go from one person's thoughts to another's mind. The body decays underground, and the thoughts remain without home, without custodian, and without thinking, which makes them want to erupt because there are no longer any word-shaped containers, pouring down on people in the form of natural disasters or diseases.

"Thus, the art of digging for stories and placing them in exquisitely decorated words is a job protecting human beings. You see, darling, that the angel writer can still negate a defeat through witty stories so that he does not commit *seppuku*[2] like the Japanese you so admire."

I tell her all this after she has come and taken a pose of solitude, her head in her hands, unable to decide whether to

---

[2] Seppuku or harakiri is the medieval Japanese custom among samurais of committing ceremonial suicide.

stay with me and be transformed into a memory someday, different from herself and unrecognizable, or to run away from home and live like every other real person.

It looks like she has understood – I am at sea.

Love as Grounds for Murder

The appearance of that milky cloud was a surprise. He could not recall how he had ended up catching sight of the advancing dawn. He would sleep under the window and, from where he lay, he could see a part of the sky from where light would rise and spread out over the city. Morning would usually come instantaneously. He would sleep half awake and then jump up to see that the sky was already bright; light had arrived.

The coarseness of his body separated him from the outside world. He put his feet on the cold floor, walked up to the open window, and held out his palm. He could feel the wind. He could not see the road but could hear the sound of the cars, while his feet sucked in the chill of the wooden floor. It remained deep within him, nonetheless. His introspective mood would multiply and spread out over the other hours of the day. His body would thicken upon itself and distance itself even further from what it absorbed of the outside world. During his childhood, the outside world was within him. He had never felt the need to protect himself from it. On the contrary, he sought opportunities to flee from home. At any time, even when he was at home, he would keep the outside within himself. Despite this, he was certain that the dryness of his body was not a product of his age.

The sky above his head was the body of a newborn baby – still azure and soft, with transparent capillaries spreading the color blue. There were places at that particular time when, with the sky still delicate and developing, cannons were fired upward to crack open a path for the light.

There was a crackling breath inside it, from his nose to his throat and then on to his lungs. In some places, it came from her moaning, from the sounds of her unintelligible words. And when his breath went back out, the same thing happened – she tried to speak. Her words never carried any meaning; they would simply pour out from his mouth and nostrils. Marie would constantly show signs of her presence. Perhaps the hardening of his body was connected to her. (This thought had crossed his mind infinite times.) Marie was erecting a wall within him so that only she would remain and then speak clearly. She kept devouring his body slowly. She had found his weak spot and had risen like that cloud of light and was spreading within his body, physically transforming him.

In the following days, it became clear that his body was now going to belong to Marie.

This manifested clearly in several ways. It started at a café. (Perhaps she had grabbed on to him early on, but the unusual side of it took shape before the eyes of strangers, and this made it noticeable to him as well.) When his friends were chatting, the three of them stared at him for a moment. He unhurriedly lowered the napkin from his lips, crushed it, then opened his palm, placed the napkin on the table, smoothed it with his palm, and got to his feet with just two words, "I'm leaving."

One of them had later said that he had been cleaning his lips with the napkin for a long time, which was unusual. He had dabbed his upper lip delicately while biting the lower one at the same time. Then he had once again gracefully moved the napkin back and forth, kissing it ever so slightly, almost unnoticeably. He had continued caressing his lips like a woman that was far away…

This incident had been compounded by others. When you pour a dye into a jar of water and watch how it dissolves, you see the color sinking to the bottom with full force and then pause for a few seconds before branching out into the water and dissolving with the hebetude of a dying snake. Marie had set a similar trap inside him – he had no way of escaping if the trap was his own body, in which she was dissolving.

Perhaps he had kept quiet about her for too long and that was why his body was mutating, but people around the world would fall in love and then grow apart, live in a state of depression for a few months, perhaps years, and then there would come a time when that love would rot and turn into a memory. Something different had been happening to him. Marie had overcome the stage of rotting and, irrespective of what he wanted, she was not just seeking rebirth but taking form as a woman while suffocating his manhood, replacing it with her own being.

On his way back home from work, he would pay hookers from the streets in an attempt to find his manhood this way and prove to himself that his body was capable of loving other women besides Marie. He would roar and grunt the first couple of minutes, moving his naked body one way and another before crashing down on them. His head would first land on the woman's shoulder. Then his knees would buckle, and then his whole body would shatter. They would feel his suffering, perhaps because women of the street never betray their first love. They spread themselves before men but they leave their bodies as if constrained by strait jackets, and their dreamy eyes stare at the ceiling. They allowed his body to crash into theirs and cause pain so that it could collapse like a badly structured skyscraper.

He needed to find his earlier firmness but also wanted to hear Marie's shapeless words which still sounded like sighing and moaning. He disgusted himself, but none of it helped. He was transforming into her with every hour, while she was far away, suspecting nothing of his inhuman experience, perhaps taking a walk, holding her children's hands.

He got to know some other women, urged on by the stupid logic that he had to 'forget her.' They would open up to him about themselves, telling him about past lovers, disappointments, failed attempts at suicide, being misunderstood by their parents, and other minutiae. The more they spoke, the more they walked past him with their naked and virgin souls, turning into defenseless gas balloons that could come across a pin around any corner. He was caring towards those women. He would even watch them raise their feet for the small step from the street to the sidewalk. They had simply rolled into the center of his attention because they had told him about themselves all the way to the very bottom. They had ended up beneath his wing, touched him, and reached his lips. But all this had become tedious and he would say to himself, *Perhaps everyone grows tired of a woman that is incapable of escaping...*

Marie could leave at any moment, and it was this fear that had given birth to love.

He needed something big to bring back his manhood. He had been taught from childhood that if his strength was not going to be enough in a fight, he would need to use a knife or to perhaps use a stone to bash his opponent's head. He did not even know how to kill himself. He decided to kill someone, but the idea was not convincing. Would she leave him or would she mourn like a woman and produce tears in his eyes?

If he could survive the transformation... he could wait, perhaps isolate from the whole world, so that he could relive the delicate movements she would make – the way she combed her hair, sitting at the mirror, her shoulders oblivious and drooping, how she would forget why she had gathered her hair, and that desperate glance she cast at her reflection. That was what Marie would do – that young but pensive woman. He would encourage himself, *Be patient, until all this melds into your body and she, full of yearning, speaks within you.*

Diseased Words

This chapter is dedicated to those who entrusted their love to me before they left.

I tried to ignore it for four days – that happens when you look away from the sharp gaze of a madman. But there is no way out – there's something wrong with the word 'leaving.' Perhaps I have made it fall ill. I had never thought too much about traveling, going, or moving. There had been fleeting exposures to advertising about coastal cities or mountain lodges on travel brochures but nothing else; that is, I had no particular way of knowing when and how that word which had invaded my calm for several days had been infected with disease.

In my mind, the word 'leaving' is slamming itself from wall to wall, giving birth to synonyms like 'getting the hell out.' My past experience suggests that continuing this would lead to misfortune (disgust by other people, being confined to a hospital ward for months, and, importantly, being unable to visit her…) and the word amputation room is what I see in my head, which is what I was avoiding. When I was a child, I had taken some words there and they had been cut and removed from my head. I banish thoughts about that removal process and give myself hope, thinking, *This will pass. Have patience.*

'Leaving' as a word is a dangerous thing; the little screens on the streets, in homes, and everywhere else alert us to the means being used to combat diseased words and warn us particularly about the surprising cunning and lethal danger posed by 'leaving.'

Leaving also gives birth to separating, and I am increasingly withdrawing from people. I feel a sense of unrest. My movements differ from the usual ones – skipping, rushing, and suddenly stopping. These things will betray me. Before I go out of the house, I make an effort to walk at the same uniform pace as everyone else. I turn on the little screen and recall the moving images of walking meant for children. I measure my movements again, one foot to the other, a distance of thirty cm, a pace of four hundred meters in twelve minutes. All this is so that people move in the same way and do not inconvenience each other with surprises because societal thinking is almost the same, while diseased words invade and distort this monotony. I leaped out of bed in the morning towards the door, one arm through a shirt and the shoes on my feet throwing me out of the house. I was running fast; images around me were blending into each other – the green light of a pharmacy, a red dress, hands that left a trace behind them in the air… (running thirty km an hour with fragmented thinking – stone-cat-human, without colors or analysis, my vision unable to look within my eyes). *Because when I miss you in my dreams and jump awake like a snake has bitten me, I run so that my vision cannot digest what is around me.*

Two women are talking, their gazes unblinking, staring into each other's eyes without looking around. It is possible to talk only in this way; if you look around and cast your eyes on another occurrence or item and continue to talk, the other person will immediately notice this and contact Wisdom Hall. I try to walk past unnoticed. I slow down my run and equalize my pace with theirs as if through an agreement. They are silent and stare right into my eyes, unsmiling and unliving. I think that all the diseased words have been removed from them, leaving only yes and no. There are so many empty-headed people now that my body starts to shudder. I cover myself from their stares with my palms and continue to walk haphazardly. "Young man!" one of them shouts, and the other says, "Behave yourself." Faster, I advance unnaturally. They take out the little screens from their purses and photograph me. I have been hunted. I tell myself, *I am being pursued,* and I flee without turning back...

I wait, I restrain myself, I think of her on the days when I go to the swimming pool, and I learn to cry underwater so that nobody notices. If only Sunday would come sooner, it will be two months that she's in that hospital room, and family members are allowed to visit every Sunday. In order to keep the infection from spreading, the patients are kept separated by glass, and you cannot hear each other's voices.

"You must come," she had said before being betrayed. "Bring your mouth close to the glass and fog it up, but make sure the doctors don't notice. Then you should draw a few curly waves. I'll see them," she said. "I'll recall my word again... Don't get caught," she said. "Whatever happens, don't get caught so that you can remind me..."

Since she is not at my side, the word that is so dear to us is easy to hide. How can I tell her that over the past two months, I have put so much pressure on that ailing word, clamped it down that others have come, and spread around in my mind, and 'leaving' has moved from them to the others. They are wandering freely in my head, spreading through my uncombed hair, appearing in each movement of my body. It has no fear. It does not submit to the clamp. I catch it in my mind and press it to the wall and bleed it dry, but it slips away again, collects its synonyms and goes on the offensive. Foolish word! It doesn't even know that I am striving to protect it because otherwise, those in the word amputation room will catch it and humiliate it, split it up letter by letter, and eliminate it. Sometimes, I lie down and grab my head in my hands, rub my temples, and as soon as I sense that 'leaving' is there, I talk to it, persuade it to remain hidden, and explain that it was born of someone else, that it has come forth from the main words she and I had, which we had cherished and concealed for years. Had it now come and wanted to betray that word we loved?

"My heart has already been robbed once," she would say. "They stormed in and snatched it, scratching at my veins as they were leaving. Don't forget the waves…"

I gradually realize that the word 'leaving' is a traitor. Doing the bidding of the word amputation room, it had come with its synonyms to separate me from the word she had given. What should I do? I lie down and ponder this, slowly killing my body where it has settled down and is trying to elicit movements of departure. Today, I kill one of my legs. I bend it and place it beneath me. It goes numb, but there is a dancing man in my mind whose movements are black. My elbows, knees, and all the connections are cut and neglected. I make myself dance so that there will be sparks in the darkness – shreds of light are produced that search for the word she left behind. In this monotonous city, 'leaving' and its mechanisms, its synonyms like 'heading out,' are leading me to ruin.

When we walk about with her in the city, I would say whenever we came across an elderly man, "You will go before us and blink at us so that you can show this in the sky."

And we would hold each other as if facing a camera, and we would look into the old man's eyes (In my mind, I saw her, islands, the hut in the woods, and...) and blink. We would be photographed from all sides. We would be in the world of devices that poured out light. All of our images would be displayed up above. We have an album of pictures in the sky. Nothing is forgotten because people are only occupied with photographing us and dying before us, obsessed with taking this to the other side quickly.

It's Sunday. There is a crowd in the word amputation room. The medical staff is handing out papers to everyone. People are writing their diseased words in those forms and waiting for their names to be called out. The elderly are sitting, their heads hanging along the wall, the younger ones are standing near the window grills, and there are sounds of crying coming from the children's room. Suddenly, the door slams open against the wall and a young girl runs out, crying and falling down next to me. I put my arms around her and raise her up from the floor. She shivers as she shows me the wrinkled paper in her palms with the words, "Red moon." So the child had seen a reddish moon, found this intriguing, and remembered it, and the moon had brought forth new synonyms and taken the girl to a world of fairytales. Her parents had sensed the influence of the diseased word and had brought her to the word amputation room. Her mother walks up, takes the child from my embrace, and her eyes catch the word on my paper – 'leaving.' Holding her daughter tightly, she fearfully slips back into the children's room.

I don't see her this Sunday because the photograph that the women took in the street has achieved its objective. I have been brought to the word amputation center. As they connect the devices to my head and turn them on, checking my response rhythm through moving images, I sleep peacefully because I have nothing to fear. They are going to find 'leaving,' the word they created themselves – bloodied, murdered, it had failed to reach the word she had concealed…

The following day, suppressing an expression of joy, monitoring the distance my feet are supposed to keep from each other, thirty cm, I rush to welcome her. She is holding the hand of a man wearing the amputation room uniform, half leaning on his shoulder. I walk up to her and say hello. We cannot talk properly while that fiend is next to her. She says they are getting married, that I should congratulate them. I hold her hand as if to congratulate her and press it tightly in a way that her fingers are shaped like a wave. I attract her gaze to those waves, but she is blank. The official looks closely and stares directly into my eyes. It is time to go. What we had given birth to together has now been removed from her, but she has managed to implant that diseased word inside me…

He Died and Did Not
Take God with Him

It is a lie that the blinds do not see. Their gaze is toward their own eyelids.

On the sixth day, God ended his work of creation and rested on the seventh day and called it sacred, but on the eighth day, His calm was broken because...

I think that Adam and Eve were making love in God's dream, afraid of awakening Him as they twisted and made caveman sounds. Adam fell into a deep sleep such that Eve could be created, and so Adam was in God's dream, and Eve was in Adam's. Thus, she was created after passing through two hot dreams (a common process as described in the Zhuangzhi[3] – a dream within a dream). She got to her feet. I think she had some soil pressed in her palm so that she could turn human and the soil was the material that provided balance (which means that balance has a material basis). What did Eve think when she saw a man next to her? That, which God saw in His dream, as did Adam. These two

---

[3] The original footnote is missing. Here it is again – A Chinese philosophical piece, approximately 4th century B.C.

were docile in their thinking, because their minds had been enslaved and were in chains. The key to their freedom was the snake, and the forbidden fruit was the only way out – at any moment, they were going to step outside the dream. (The snake was fascinated with the view because it was Juliet's kind nurse[4], Woland[5], and Mephistopheles[6] – the characters that help the young lovers). *"... They sewed fig leaves together and made coverings for themselves."*[7] They were preparing to leave when Adam heard God's footsteps, and they were afraid, so they hid themselves, and God (in His own dream) called out, "Adam, Adam..." Seeing that they had found the way out of the dream, it was true that He had grown angry that He would no longer be able to joke with them, play hide-and-seek, and so on, but He nonetheless banished them from his dream, which was paradise. Finally, the lovers moved from the world of white shadows to the Earth and began to have dreams of their own where they saw God, who was growing more and more irritable as a result...

Adam and Eve perished and they took the secret of the dream with them. Perhaps, as I write this, I am also a part of His brief daytime nap. When I go to buy shoes, I bend the soles and examine them fastidiously so that I can leap out of God's dream in firm heels.

The only way out of a dream is the brief state of staring or riveting one's gaze, where I see things only from my

---

[4] W. Shakespeare, *Romeo and Juliet*

[5] M. Bulgakov, *The Master and Margarita*

[6] W. Goethe, *Faust*

[7] The book of Genesis, the first chapter in the Bible.

point of view and find it difficult to notice the other happenings in the room. I constantly take and place myself in a dance circle. It's like a hurricane. As soon as I try to examine Him, I am called, perhaps even hypnotized, (One cannot rule that out.) and thrown into another dream which occurs in that same great dream. That's the bad thing about the universe – there is no other. Since anything and everything that is considered to be something else is simply some other thing in the same universe, and there is thus no other, it is fake.

David[8] the Invincible said that there are things that our consciousness creates, like the *aralez*[9], and there are things that are true, that we can touch, like a deer. I am a creation of the Almighty and I am not something He can touch, just like the *aralez* is for me. Knowing this, and even assuming that He is playing with me again, putting these thoughts in His dream into a delusional mind like mine, I nonetheless close my eyes, plug my ears, and hide my tactile surfaces, especially the tips of my fingers which go into my fists so that I do not ask Him any questions and so that He does not open the doors of the dream again, and I am not deceived into leaping out with joy as if I had managed to appear in another one.

God knows us, yes indeed. He knows you, me, the plates and curtains, the glasses, and every small step taken by ants. He knows my crow named Markos, the diameter of

---

[8] An Armenian philosopher of the V-VI centuries

[9] Dog-like creatures, or spirits, in Armenian cultural beliefs or in the Armenian mythology, who live in the sky, or on Mount Ararat, according to some versions.

its cage, and… everyone, but I continue enumerating them and grow dully happy at my appearance in other dreams.

So who was the Devil anyway? Perhaps the one that managed to escape the great dream and create another one – one that belonged to him, one that did not have the universe?

I will henceforth go against the lord of the dream and the devil as well, who did not give us freedom by falling to the Earth but rather tried to involve us, in turn, in the amusing dreams of his own creation. And I disfigure my body, producing clownish movements. I wear a cap that covers my face. I dress in black and step into the shadows at night to deprive myself of my body. I turn into one of those beggars so that the Christ and the anti-Christ do not recognize me, do not catch me, and do not bring me back into that character that walks unrealistically and smiles unnaturally.

They say that blind people cannot see. I don't believe it. Like the blind, I too have a gaze that is turned towards my eyelids. I am one of them and, if need be, I can be a saint or the most sordid of sinners as long as I get to be an individual – another outside this universe – and I get to enjoy, as part of my own dream, the dreams of the lords of the heaven and the Earth and those lords as well. I'll make them ride bicycles and smoke one of Arturo's cigars[10], all to allow myself some unrestrained fun…

If the Lord existed one second before I was born – and I believe this is the case (Books and people from a thousand years ago have spoken about Him.) – and if He will remain

---

[10] Arturo Fuente cigars, produced since 1912.

a second after my death – and I believe He will continue to do so – then it is not I that will take Him with me. He was, is, and will be. "God is dead."[11] The wise ones that killed him off have died, but He remained and is perhaps alive (for the time being), and I have no desire to attempt murder, because I am in His dream where I am but a shadow. This is why I am in a rush to die. It is so that when I achieve the age of wisdom, He is unable to find me and expose me for the puppet that I am.

I am the one He did not create, the one that named the first ones in the plural, irrespective of the Adams, Kingus, Purushas, Ymirs, Keyumars, Phoroneuses, and Batetas[12] from a completely different reality where nobody existed before or after me. I am a drop of the sea that distinguishes itself from the universal color of the ocean and its uniform density. I am covered by the color of the sea and my weight is my Achilles's heel (My only weakness in the sea is the weight of my drop.) that may betray me, which is why I wrap myself around a woman, and she only takes my phallus inside and hides it, but even that is salvation. They come, weigh me, and do not recognize the fugitive; the woman, Lilith[13], will not betray me. She will open up her womb for eternity to accept a drop of me inside and I will lose this weight so that the heavenly and the Earthly cannot catch me and cast me back into their dreams. From now on, everything will come forth in my own dream. The scene

---

[11] F. Nietzsche, *The Gay Science*

[12] The first human beings according to different religious traditions, beliefs, and legends.

[13] The wife of Adam, according to Kabbalist Theosophy.

cannot take me into its wholeness in order to sense me, and I am victorious over the knowledge that I can be noticed there against my will. From now on, I am a creator that looks at the world as one would look at a painting on a canvas, separate from oneself.

I think that the secret of Adam and Eve's freedom has been discovered. They made love – or, in the language of paradise, they ate clouds and managed to lose some of their weight for a few minutes, thus remaining unrecognized. Perhaps they managed, during those eternal seconds, to flee the infinity of the universe, to escape His dream.

Forbidden Thinking

At the steps of the control center, my partner lines up with me and signals that he is going to bring the car around. On the way, I pick up the activity screen from him and click on the address layout program. The apartment door on the seventy-eighth floor of Skyscraper 21/4 is opened by a girl, her head hung low and her clothes a mess. She is young, but she has managed to embellish her wrists with fresh scars. Perhaps her whole body has turned into fodder for punishment. My partner pushes her into a chair and says, "Speak." We wait. I open the box. My partner takes out the chisel with the concave section and digs it into her scars. It is as if the girl is waiting for pain to start speaking calmly.

"... After leaving him, I always feel like I want to curl up. I walk and see my smooth palms swinging beside me and I miss him... My body's first decorations happened when I was crossing the street and the oncoming cars did not yield. Then a boiling egg was slamming itself against the walls of the pot. The chick did not want to boil and broke through the shell, trying to jump out of the pot..."

She stops, my partner bends over and brings the surgical microscope to within a millimeter of her eyes – 1, 2, 3, 4, 5, 6, 7… As soon as the chronometer in his palm beeps, he says, "That's all." He straightens his back, turns off the voice recorder hanging from his neck, and gives me the chronometer he has been holding. Even before making it to the threshold, I hear the strangled vomiting, usually a disgusting scene, and the sounds remind me of the surgical factory at the center.

In the elevator, my partner tells me, "If all of them speak like this one, submitting to the very first tool, then we'll have a lot less to do on the job; it will lighten our workload."

"As long as we don't meet a perceiver," I respond to him as I turn on the screen and we speed to our next address.

Perceivers are rare. Besides their own reserves, they listen to the unusual stories of others and keep them tightly concealed. People seek out a perceiver and then talk freely so that their thinking could somehow be saved from the center.

I stop the car in a suburb and walk towards Structure 32/1. Some people have gathered near the house, one of them rushing in my direction and saying that he is the one who had called in the story concealer. Spotting us, one of the people gathered in the yard slips away, and my partner says, "Remember that one…"

I was a junior assistant. I hadn't yet managed to make a perceiver talk. My partner would tell me all kinds of legends about them, but the fact was that they would resist until their last breath. They would be taken to the main room at the center where high society gathered. This was where perceivers gave in. Further concealment would be foolish.

We enter the house and the members of the family lead us to the living room, where a table has been placed behind a man's back and he is awkwardly tied to it. We invite the curious bystanders out, turn on the recorder, and say, "Speak." The man is quiet. My partner gestures with his fingers and I open the toolbox. I hand him the surgical scalpel and he slowly pierces the man's earlobe. He screams but does not speak, and my partner says, "Perhaps we should take him to the center." The man shakes his head no – the snot hanging from his nose extending and then contracting like an earthworm – because he has already started to speak.

"... A grayish velvety blue had spread over the roofs of the buildings. I looked at that moist color that glued together the frightening thoughts in my mind; my misery and the sky were the same color that day... There is a woman with whom you must live in your country, where you are, with a familial love, the kind that leads to childbirth, and then there is the love of leaving, the love of escaping with you..."

The man finishes and my partner turns off the device. We call the family members and order them not to untie him until he has vomited. I remind my partner of the person that slipped away and he says:

"If he had been thinking, then his thoughts hadn't reached his throat yet. Let them accumulate – his family members or one of his acquaintances will report him. Thinking is like an itch – it starts at the crown of your head but, like an idiot, you put your back to a hard surface and scratch hard, until your skin comes off and the red flesh is visible below. But you fail to understand whether you were scratching your itch or the itch of your itch…"

He agitatedly runs a finger across his abdomen, where he keeps an old scar.

The technical crew follows us in. They turn on the electronic devices in the patient's house – the phones, tablets, bean-sized screens, televisions, and all remote-controlled appliances. They calibrate the computers, restore the deleted social network pages, and recall their photographs and external activities. They tear off the posters stuck to the walls and put up advertisements about new robot models. If the patient has any old books, they remove them and replace them with moving pictures, for example, Anna Karenina smiling enigmatically on the first page, skipping around with her child in the next image, a young man glancing at her through a crack in the door, one with her pulling at her hair as a sign of despair and then the station on Page Four, the train tracks and Karenina's blood in bubbles.

As soon as the workday is over, I head home and throw myself into bed, exhausted. I wake up from a hissing in my ear and she is startled. She smiles anxiously, her palms covering the lips she constantly bites. She is a 'patient.' My ear has not gotten over her whispering and keeps brewing the basic sounds she is making. I am an animal startled by the rustling, and I look in the direction of the danger – at her.

I had told her many times that if she felt like she was falling ill, she should ask for our services through her own freewill, and that would give her the right to choose her own listener. She could ask for a woman or, even better, prefer a child. That would cause less suffering.

She would say, "Don't worry. If I fall ill, I'll find a listener for myself…"

She meant a perceiver and that always made me angry. It would be a knife in the back. Perhaps it would make me ill in turn. We were young, but we were coldhearted in our pleasures and emotions, so our bodies were both pure, with no scars or extinguished injuries.

I had seen the tattered breasts of women, young ladies with mangled faces, and I had dragged their scars into her body and flung myself into the bathroom to do vomiting exercises so that the worthless thinking would not begin.

I lean back on the pillow and pull her pretty body toward me, her eyes blank and her lips half-open and fluttering. These are signs I saw every day – she is weak. Her eyes are leaving – I mean, they are still in their sockets, but I can see her vision blurring because her thinking is boiling like rocks in an overflowing river. I wrap one hand around her wrist like a chain. She does not resist, and I grab her neck with the other and open her eyelids. They are moist and red on the other side – there is no longer any doubt. When tears accumulate behind one's eyelids, it means the thinking has begun. "Don't look into my eyes," she says. "I don't want you to fall ill."

I leave her half-naked and put on my clothes. Before leaving, I turn around. She is lying in the same position. Someone with my experience cannot miss the accumulation of tears, which started insignificantly small like molecules, but they have now fused together. Her eyelashes are tightly shut to hold them in, but you cannot use grains of sand to stop a river from flowing.

An unpleasant scene – I am heading to a nightclub so that I can find myself again. Like a bird pecking away for a crumb or two, it must have taken a lot of effort to make sure that the people on the street would not notice her thoughts – focused concentration, the constant need to turn her head this way, and to avoid stones being thrown at her. I decide not to call her in myself. It does not matter. One of the neighbors or her girlfriends would report her anyway. But then I would be seen as ineffective and would be stripped of my position or moved to the children's room where I would have to write down the things bawled and screamed constantly by women in labor and torture the little ones so that they would empty out every day, giving them instructions to never retain anything and do not start thinking or questioning.

My ears continue to wail. I had not done my vomiting exercises that day. If you let your concentration slip, the sounds are absorbed and turn into words. "You are a perceiver..." I can clearly put together her mumbling.

Before new perceivers guess the right type of personality, they are either caught by someone from the center or perhaps end up never fully understanding the mental state of the person they have chosen. But the experienced ones choose the path of torture to the point of being bled dry. After collecting the stories extracted from regular people into their recorders, the senior agents take these to the center. In the case of perceivers, however, it is the individual that gets dragged there so that the elite can enjoy the words moist with fresh blood and sobs right from the perceiver's mouth.

I keep shifting in my seat in the car so that I could see the outside world as it twisted by and her words could drop out of my heart and into another organ. If I could, I would have hung upside down from the ceiling handles.

"When you look into my eyes while thinking, I get dizzy. Don't look at me. I'm the type that prefers escape," her voice wheezes out of my lungs.

"You are a perceiver…" her words spread inside me, trying to infect me because I recalled once again how I would visit my father's home during my internship. In order to check whether I had kept my guard up, my senior colleague had followed me and placed an order for us from my parents' address.

We walked into the house. The wounds on my mother's cheeks had not yet scarred and she already had signs of illness. Her lids had slightly puffed. She took us to my father's study where my brothers had tied him down and awaited us. My father was foaming at the mouth. My colleague bent over him and said, "Speak." I opened the suitcase on the ground and started to work with one tool after another. When we had cut open his abdomen with a scalpel and his intestines were rubbing against my knee, my father spoke with a moan.

"… I had uncovered the bed and gotten in but kept plucking blond hairs all night from my ears, legs, and fingers. She had taken them from her hair and, secretly from me, she had planted them all over the bed in an attempt to seduce and excite my young body… A drop that had built up at the mouth of a closed tap, ready to drip, and the bang that is sounded in the brain as the hanging drop continues to gather…"

As soon as he went silent, I used the microscope to make sure that he was no longer hiding anything. I pressed the chronometer button and looked into his eyes. They were like a window that had been drenched by raindrops.

The paramedics were waiting on the other side of the door. They went in as soon as we had finished our work. I found a suitable moment and told my mother to do vomiting exercises, to stand in the sun for a long time so that her head numbs and the thinking weakens and dies. She was a powerful woman, stronger-willed than my father, so she would have spoken even later. I would have ended up being an orphan forever. In the car, I learned that they had been unable to save my father. My partner consoled me:

"What can I say? He was resisting like the will of a perceiver had taken over him."

Perhaps he was, but it was clear to me. My father spoke for a long time. He resisted because of his pride. It was so that nobody at work could say that my father spoke before his veins were cut.

When I was a child, I would frequently have nosebleeds. My parents would place me between them and give me hope, saying, "It's all right." The blood flowing out was the portion that had avoided the knives. My father breathed, a cold mountain wind from the north blowing as he exhaled, the dull sounds of the storm blending with the howling of wolves, sometimes the screeching of owls, the rustling of branches, and the momentary stamping of the feet of little beasts climbing up trees or burying into the soil to escape danger. My mother was blowing into a hot air balloon and rising up and down, sometimes breathing deeply and attracting the squawking of birds and then burying deep into the clouds and gradually extinguishing. I would go to the instinctive bellies of the seas, forests, and the sky. They would wrap themselves around me at night and moan with concern like lions that had not hunted for days or animals that were thirsty in a drought, until I recovered.

If only my father's thinking had been milder!

There are spies from the center everywhere – they are called 'earporters.' The religious communities have shown particular progressiveness. Their pastors communicate the scriptures through emotional speech and cast seeds of thinking into the souls of their congregants. As if this is not enough, they unburden our services by pulling out the thinking that is still embryonic. Unformed thinking is olfactory and sensory. It has no structure, it consists simply of horrors or interesting scenes that feed one's dreams, but that is exactly what grows later and turns into thinking, which is why the pastors kill them why they are still submerged in dark waters, just like a baby is cut apart during an abortion.

Through a new program by the center, we are going to have offices in various workplaces so that we can cut costs and take care of cases on site. They have produced a list of devices and machines for those offices using a reprint of hospital surgical equipment, which is the most convenient approach. As experts, we have been asked to examine this list and let them know if anything is missing. It includes a set of small surgical instruments (scales, scissors, lancets, surgical needles, and suturing material), clamps to arrest bleeding, surgical hammers, tools for plaster casts, vacuum immobilizers, rubber trays, emergency medical kits, a universal surgical table, tool cabinet, and stretcher, etc.

I discuss the list with her. I want to add my preferred instrument – the scalpel – but she speaks in defense of using a lancet. Finally, we end up writing both and send it by post to the center.

When I return home, she is not there. *Good,* I say to myself. It would be good for her to stay away for a while, although I know I was going to roll out of bed and search for her the very next day. It is critical to do the center's routine immediately after waking up – vomiting exercises first of all, then submerging in a swimming pool while holding one's breath, and opening and closing one's eyes underwater so that the tear microbes are washed away. *No, she would not listen to me.*

I wake up and she is in the rocking chair, with a cat in her lap. Blood from the surgical wound on her wrist has rubbed off on the cat's fur. She is holding the cat's mouth close to her face and they are licking each other as the red flows from her wrist to the crease of her elbow and glistens as it grows. While I change her bandage, she and the cat lick me. I fail at doing the exercises in the bathroom. The smell of her blood rises from my fingers to my nose and then, twisting to the top of my head, spreads across my body. I wonder what instrument the center workers had used to cut her wrist, perhaps a shaving razor or… her first wound…

I fail at doing the exercises.

I get to work and we race to a distant village. The gardener has been tied to a tree. His fellow villagers have smashed his face. We drive them off with difficulty. Everyone is shouting that the lowlife is harboring thoughts. We walk up to him and get to work. Because I'm a candidate for seniority, my partner is the one handing the instruments this time. I say to the old man, "Speak." He is silent. (A burning sensation runs beneath my eyelids, barely noticeable, but it worries me). The old man is quiet. I use forceps to push his soiled finger against his nail. He could not care less. My partner winks because he knows the weaknesses of those naïve types. He takes out a saw from the toolbox and holds it against a tree and then instructs the others to follow suit. People take up positions at each tree trunk with axes, adzes, and saws in hand. Two or three small boys even hold stones.

"Cut them down!" my partner shouts. The old man starts to cry and I hold up a hand to signal that the crowd should stop and turn on the recorder because the man has started to speak.

"... People were losing things in the snow, or, particularly during the first snowfall, they kept finding things on the white surface. Sometimes the snow makes you a loser. Sometimes it turns you into a finder when it reveals something dropped by someone else. I've grown old, but I've never been given the role of a finder..."

My partner and I are arranging our instruments and watching the technical team connect the old man's greenhouse to their screens and repair the advertising spaces on the tree trunks. My partner says that when hunting for game, it is a normal practice to hide in wait and fire a surprise shot and then come out of the shelter and follow the animal's tracks. At first, it might seem like you missed, but a short distance later, you notice the drops of blood and need to rush after the creature and catch it before it falls, reaching it before the heartbeat that signals the end of the injured body, when the blood drives the animal insane. You have to get to it and look it in the eyes. The same holds true for us. If an individual refuses the order to speak, we torture them, and the result is more satisfying because the flowing blood causes insanity as it bursts through the open wound and the person speaks, thinking that death has arrived. He says everything he kept in his heart, which is all we need. Naturally, we disinfect the wound and close it. If there is too much thinking and we are unable to keep up, the person dies, depending on the kind of case it is. If it is a recurring case and there are many wounds, there is nothing else for us to do. We usually cut open a vein and lose the patient immediately. The elite at the center do not encourage this approach because the patient's thinking remains unfinished or ends up being a bunch of snorts.

"At the center, they don't like it when they have to lean towards the recorder and try to sort out the words better," I say. My partner does not respond and takes out a small screen from his pocket, tapping on the next address.

I have been distracted when I spill those words of criticism regarding the center. I think, *Did I really say that? Perhaps that is a result of the pathological thinking that she has produced...*

There is a row of people on the ninety-first floor and the door to Apartment Six is open. A couple with funereal faces is at the doorstep. They take us to the children's room, which is a mess. D-11 images of toys have spilled out of the shattered screen and broken robots are lying everywhere. The child has been tied with his arms held tightly against his chest and he has peed his pants in fear. My partner takes four steady steps and, standing at attention, says, "Speak." The child whines but does not speak, so I open the toolbox. I pick up something... The child begins to speak without pausing for breath.

"... I killed a field mouse and asked it questions. Whose hands are the ones that finally cause worn out bills of money to crumble? Do you like to breathe? So do I – we have something in common. How many layers of smile does the sun produce in a day for its rays to be able to reach us? What would a witch do if it stepped out of the pages of fairytales and on to the streets of our megapolis? How many staring eyes can I count till evening? In what direction are they looking? What does the mouth of my bottom say?"

After finishing up, I enter their bathroom and puncture my thumb with a razor, pressing out a gob of blood. No blood has come from my nose or any other place for a long time and I am afraid that some thinking has already sucked up my outer blood from the inside. She is of the generation of wandering dervishes. There are small bulges beneath her nails – whatever she has found outside, her nails have gathered beneath them. She picks at and pokes the beautiful mounds of dirt – fragments of leaves and burned soil. I love the pit of her navel, from where I remove crumbs and examine them under a microscope. The navel attracts dirt from every corner of her body. I examine the extracts of her nails and navel, and this allows me to guess her day-to-day routine.

"I'll open a space for us in your mind and I'll wait for you. It isn't easy to plow into the thoughts of someone busy with mind hunting, to break into it and sit there, until you notice me…" she said.

I take her outside the town, to a relaxation spa, so that her head could get some sun and emptiness-pumping sessions. She calls me before the fifth day and says all kinds of strange things.

"Do you remember my childhood door that had become my dog? I would rub it gently as I closed it and pretended to run and hide under the blanket from its growling?"

"Yeah, you've told me about it. Keep sticking to your treatment. That's enough." I turn off the screen. It is one of her weaknesses. To this day, whenever she sees an old door, she would place some water next to it, saying that it was whining and it must be thirsty…

I do not get any news from her for almost a month. Then I am called to the center in the middle of the night, given her name, and told to go to the spa.

I get there at the moment when her body is lying there covered in blood. My partners from the center seem tired. They have pricked her body with awls but only managed to extract dull sounds from her. Her head is already half turned and downcast, but my unusual imagination reveals to me how her cheek has turned blue and is pressed to the floor. Her lips flicker like the day when I did not wish to listen to her, and a scar has appeared on her arm. The team holds a recorder to her mouth. She is saying, "I love the perceiver…" I mechanically raise a knife to prevent her from finishing the sentence, but she stops out of exhaustion. I walk into the bathroom and look at myself in the mirror, with the knife in my hand that I was about to drive into her heart with fear in an attempt to avoid future torture like a coward. I throw the instrument aside, quickly rub my eyelids and clean them with cotton, calm down my racing heart, and take deep breaths to avoid gasping.

Her family had long left for the other side of the border where things were relatively calm and only dream-hunters operated. That was why the center had given me the order to go to the spa. It was so that I could fill in the death certificate and be present at the voice-hearing ceremony at her release.

At the office in the center, I stand on one side of the table, with three people sitting in front of me and looking into my eyes. There are wires attached to the tips of my fingers and they are connected to a verifying device, while my head is linked to detection needles. All this is for the timely prevention of pathological fears, which can be caused through infection by a family member's voice. Next to me, there are small screens with various parameters of data from my body. They turn on the screens and start the recording, and she speaks:

"… I need to feel someone breathing, the sound of someone breathing next to me so that I can blend it with the sounds of my own breath beneath my nose and create

76

different, as yet unknown, breathing notes and not feel alone... I talk hurriedly to arrange the busy day I had yesterday, and I even plan tomorrow. I am a piece of writing, a collection of various words..."

She speaks for a long time and I am resisting. But she has already bent over and screamed into me like I was a well. Her echo bounces back to my throat and drives the data needles on my screens crazy. The staff opens their boxes but I do not wait for the instruments. I start to speak because no other tool would be able to unlock my tongue the way her painful voice had.

"... This woman who is next to you is someone I care about, but she has the habit of slipping away and keeping her distance from me. That's how she was – she had a mist in her eyes, and the cold usually brings people together. I was standing at a bus stop waiting for a bus on a cold day, leaning from one foot to the other, five paces away from her. I could not decide what to do because I wanted to talk to her. I lit a cigarette and the wind took that blue mist from my mouth to her breasts and her face. As it wrapped itself in her hair, she stared at the puddles where she could see her reflection and her head was the only thing outside of that cloud of smoke. Only one lungful of smoke got to her and I saw her like a series of images in slow motion... I walked up to her in a slow, unnoticed flutter. My arm touched her and I grew warm. That was the day she saved me from freezing..."

I am now in a ramshackle village hut. I have been fired but, unlike perceiver supporters, mind-hunters are not drained of blood on the first occasion. Now, when my thinking piles up and manifests through obvious physical symptoms, I realize that someone in my circle of acquaintances will report me, and so, I contact the center first, choose a woman in the catalog and ask her to cut fresh wounds into my body as I speak about the things that have come to my head. In this way, they no longer drag me to the center and I thus avoid the happy whooping of the elite.

No matter how many scars appear on my body, she only needs a couple of days to gather enough strength and overcome the numb calmness within me. She reminds me that I am the perceiver, and we continue our resistance together.

The Snow Woman

O, greatest Buddha,
The spring took away
The image of her
From cherry tree branches.
Toshinari Hanaki

At dawn, he went about his everyday ritual. He picked up one of the half-dried balls of dough on the windowsill, crushed it in his palm, and threw it out. A flock of sparrows covered it and began to peck away. He would be still as a statue on the second-floor balcony because his movements would startle the creatures. As soon as he moved his hand to crush more dough the birds would fly away in unison to the branches of the nearby cherry tree. Then, the boldest of them would return one by one, followed by the rest of the flock.

They don't trust me, thought Toshinari.

Four years ago, he had announced to his parents that he was not the same person as before (He was sure that they had already been convinced of this.) and that he would move away from them and live in solitude because he considered himself to have the destiny of a hikikomori.

During the first months of his solitude, he discovered this approach to feeding the birds, but he would be hurt and disappointed like a child by their timid behavior.

He got used to it with time. They had no basis on which to trust him. After all, when a passerby gives money to a beggar, he immediately rushes away afterwards, doesn't he? If he lingers and tries to start a conversation, this is often offensive to the beggar, who then responds rudely. Just like the animals do not trust his sudden movements, so does the beggar not trust people's words.

He crushed a dough ball and thought that he trusted the Almighty but did not speak to Him much. If He were to respond to me one day, I would not trust that voice. I would be frightened by its sound and be overcome with sorrow...

It was an amusing idea, and he finally threw the crumbs that had filled the creases in his skin. He clapped his hands together to clean them, and the sound of a slap rang out. He had placed the first lock on his heart to keep that hateful sound inside, and perhaps there had been others before that, but his memory had not preserved them.

He listened for each sound, trying to analyze its meaning. He was particularly attentive to the sounds that he could hear but could not see.

He had submitted to that habit at around the age of six when the slap that thundered from the neighboring room had stunned him, followed then by his mother's concealed gasp and his father's hoarse and soft bravado.

Toshinari would wake up at night and hear the barks and howls of the street dogs. Their snarls that sometimes led to a whimper from one of them would stop just as suddenly as they started. At times like that, he pictured – or rather imagined – what was going to happen – a struggle between two packs and a wounded dog. Its whining had stopped because it was being devoured under a window somewhere in that city of Musashino.

He had experienced some internal changes during adolescence, during *Hanami*, when the blossoms had appeared in their city and the celebrations dedicated to the blooming sakura had caused a wave of delight in the people. He would see the sakura flowers every year in March, but he was going to understand the difference between two things that spring – looking at something but not digesting it and taking it no further than the lenses of his eyes or, in the other case, noticing it, feeling its image within him, and rejoicing with the whole of his spiritual being, cherishing that experience and achieving a state of awe.

Toshinari had given in to that awe. In the days that followed, he had constantly talked about it to the few acquaintances he had, as if he had witnessed a miracle which nobody would believe, as if this forced him to describe his experience in the minutest detail.

He had matured much sooner than his peers. He delicately chose comparative expressions to bring forth the awe he felt in his heart. Once, when he had fallen again into a description that was worshipping of nature, an older friend at school, Akira Tanabe, whom he considered close, exclaimed:

"You speak so delicately that it would not surprise me if we discovered that you used needles to knit warm socks in your spare time, like someone who feels cold all the time, and that woman's job is probably something you'd enjoy. Why don't you participate in the ikebana contest?" Akira was encouraged by the giggling girls. Then she left with the laughing group.

Toshinari had blushed with embarrassment. He had never before felt the taste of betrayal from up close, and his hands had balled into fists when he suddenly heard someone breathing. He turned around to see Setsuko, who was two years junior to him. She smiled and pointed to a cherry tree that was growing near the fence, and they both walked quietly to the tree. He was angry on the outside as an irresistible force urged him to follow the girl, but the sakura continued to blossom inside him.

They were not going to understand him. After the thundering slap, this was the second incident that thickened the skin that separated him from the outside, and he felt that this unknown force had tightened a rope of solitude around his neck and was pulling at the depths of his soul.

The other chain that served to separate him from society into solitude came from his ability to hear sounds. At first, the sound of the slap had caused a wave of despair, but this was followed by disgust. His hearing was so sensitive that he could even pick up sounds from the bodily functions of a person standing in front of him – the gurgling of water through a throat and the rumbling of food being digested in a stomach… This caused him nausea and a desire to escape, making him feel like he could not stand being within two paces of another human being.

Back in high school, he attempted to formulate his own theory on this. In a high-paced world where people cannot even notice their surroundings, the consumerist market surrounds everyone in a steel frame and proceeds to squeeze the vital juices out of them. Whether that frame is a triangle, a square, or a circle depends on the specific geographical characteristics of a given person. If the person wants to go in circles and return home, then that circle must adhere to the rules of the market and have no pieces from outside that frame so that the person has no way of penetrating into the depths of his own soul and discovering new worlds.

People have lost their reverence of the word – it is true materialism that makes them seek the word, which means that they only see what material is, without seeing the word that created it… And it is easier to control such people, that is, to remove the internal ability to imagine or create.

In particular, the scurrying people belonging to these new times have gained a uniform vision (which has first been instilled in them by the governing system and has then been passed on from generation to generation). The technocratic person has not looked up at the sky in months, even years, because his vision has grown used to and has been fixated on the square unit that has been allocated to him. It is right in front of him, and there is nothing 'extra' or 'additional' that has been allowed in his perception. It is simply not accepted. Toshinari was convinced that if a person were to look outside, he or she would be surprised, perhaps to the point of panic and even suicide.

But he resisted that and grew worthy of the blessing of nature…

***

Toshinari, locked in his twenty-three-square-meter apartment, studied traditions. This kept his mind awake and, most importantly, would help him discover the three words of which he dreamed.

Before death, every hikikomori was required to leave three words behind for a younger person that had just taken a first step on that descending path. Those few words pronounced by the more experienced (if one could use the word in this case) hikikomori before their rebirth were special signs that the followers into solitude could use as keys to discover the mental secrets of their predecessor. These three words were sometimes enough to reproduce in detail the thoughts that the other had had and even the items placed in his room, the view that was visible from his window, or the tree that he worshipped because every hikimori rented a place positioned near a tree. In any case, Toshinari had heard all this back when he was an adolescent. Perhaps these were legends, but he was very interested in the hidden world contained in these words of legacy.

The words passed down were kept by the new generation as the most sacred of items if the person was deemed worthy. One day, a stranger would knock on their door and hand over an envelope with the sacramental envelope...

He had not yet received the blessed words from the previous generation of hikikomori, even though he was on the threshold of his fifth year. During those five years, he had never stepped outside his apartment, nor allowed any external agent into his, so that his tranquility would not be disturbed. It was only the images on the other side of his window that greeted him as a television would in a normal family. On Thursdays, the food delivery person would visit, and sometimes the postman would come with the books he had ordered. They would not cross the threshold of his place because everyone would know in advance that the apartment they were visiting housed a hikikomori and they knew that any unnecessary questions would be deemed offensive. Toshinari would not look in the direction of their face in order to avoid any sparks of affection from eye-to-eye contact. He would open the door and take the package of food or the books, staring all the while in the direction of the feet in front of him. Sometimes, he would sketch and recreate the thousands of shoes he had seen. Toshinari didn't know that they were surprisingly similar to the faces of the people that wore them.

Over the past months, he was submerged in the analysis of the character called *Yuki-onna* but with multiple names (the snow woman, snow girl, daughter of the night, and so on). In some places, *Yuki-onna* was depicted as a witch, while other books mentioned her white hair and readiness to help men or, on the contrary, the cruelty with which she trapped travelers in snowstorms.

His obsessions with this character became clear during a thaw when he had left his window half open and, with closed eyes, swallowed the sounds of the layers of snow disappearing. The different sounds of the thaw calmed his soul and filled him with delicate layers of sorrow. He opened his eyes a short while later and spotted a puddle that had been covered by a thin crust of ice. There was a mysterious beauty in that ice layer...

It was the beginning of March, and the frosty nights hardened the outer skin of puddles, but stray dogs would walk all over it in the morning, breaking the weak ice with their chins to have a drink of water.

Toshinari was full of unusual emotions toward that puddle as if that sensitive and delicate frost was *Yuki-onna*, and she knitted that icy surface like an intricate web for her own protection each night.

He was startled by a knock at his door. It was not the day for food deliveries, nor had he ordered any new books. Could it be…

He was frozen in place, as if not wanting to hear the rustling of clothing and the sound of the lock turning on the other side. He bowed before the book in order to embody the sounds of expectation. It seemed like the wooden flooring was creaking under advancing feet, and he bent over even further over the words before him: *"The poet Sōgi told the story of his encounter with Yuki-onna in Echigo…"* Perhaps his internal strife would calm down if he managed to read the text on the page. Toshinari did not see the approaching figure because he had turned his back to the door as he waited with bated breath. The stranger covered the distance between the door and the window and breathed down on the bone at the end of his neck. The charm of expectation vanished and was replaced by terror as the words on the paper blurred because of the water burning Toshinari's eyes. *"Sōgi described Yuki-onna as having a purely white, almost transparent body, with faint shimmers of melting snow, indescribably beautiful…"* A regular messenger would not have crossed his threshold, he was convinced of that. He did not turn to face the stranger. He was already certain that a hikikomori had died somewhere and he had been deemed worthy of the privileged words.

The envelope had been on the table for a long time. He had watched at the very edge of his field of vision how it had been placed there by a hand, transparent like a piece of ice, delicate in its features...

The paper had these words on it: *'sun,' 'cherry tree,' and 'woman.'*

He was so stunned that he copied out the words on other pieces of paper four times, but nothing changed. The word that offended him remained the same. "Woman?" Toshinari pronounced it.

How could a hikikomori leave such a word as a sacred message? After all, it led to a certain seduction that could give birth to new words.

Toshinari ran his fingers through the mess of hair on his head. And these days in particular, he thought when his mind was occupied by that accursed custom of the snow woman. How could the author of those words have felt the suffering that had taken hold of his inner being?

He looked at the dates written at the bottom, i.e. *1997 – 2019.* This was all that remained as evidence that the dead hikikomori had been real – no name, no other information that would remain a secret forever. The first year would mark the start of isolation. This was considered as a rebirth for a hikikomori, i.e. when they had separated themselves from the outside world.

And so, had this person who had withdrawn and almost achieved the peace of Buddha left the word 'woman' as a final legacy?

Toshinari was unable to sleep that night, jumping up from bed now and then, picking up the envelope from the table and reconfirming that the word was still on it. Under the moonlight, the symbol 女 seemed to take on the shape and body of a woman just as it had originally been drawn in the form of a kneeling female figure in worship…

***

The sakura had grown on the edge of the windowsill. The sunlight was held back by the iron grills and leaves that leaned on each other's lips, and all these details seemed to have the specific aim of ruining the image that appeared on the other side. But the noontime rays penetrated into the room with abundance.

Toshinari began to feed on the sun, standing for hours near the window and leaning his head at an angle that allowed the rays to fall directly on his face. His closed eyelids grew warmer, the colors glittering on the inside and forming certain images. In the early days, he was unable to find a way for the fleeing colors to gain structure. But the one thing he had working for him was time, and step by step he managed to come closer to what he was seeking – the lifestyle of the hikikomori that had left him the legacy of those words. He could now roughly see the edges of the words. The light was dense, but that adjusted itself too. Before turning his eyes to the sun, he would squeeze them tightly so that they would darken, and this would then allow the rays to slip in lightly without blinding him.

The path ahead of him would be difficult, but the pleasure and drive to disappear did not leave him with any chance for disappointment, and he was like a farsighted architect so filled with the desire to build that he could already feel the corners of the items in his mind.

All that remained was to arrange his room – his sketch of words allowed him to see a dresser with a mirror. Well, he didn't need the mirror. He had lots of light and could cover it but the couch, the cupboard next to it, and the bonsai on it, and then she suddenly appeared...

He immediately stopped his mental reconstruction that sought the dead hikikomori. He leaned his tired head, in which a school of fish seemed to be jumping around as a result of sunburn on his wrists and fell asleep.

***

Reproductions of the previous years and days had grown more frequent in Toshinari's mind. In fact, the extra crumbs of those days were more in focus, over which his life had flowed without being noticed. He had lived without holding himself accountable for it, but any life lived will be brought to account one day or another.

Until he was ten years old, cracks would appear on his skin. His whole body would start tearing itself apart. When his mother had taken him to a hospital yet again, there had been a Shinto priest in the waiting room, who had looked at his mother and said:

"Don't worry. This is the birth of a new and improved person each year."

"But I don't want this. I only want to be born from within her..." Toshinari said in a soft voice, standing near the window, as if he had to respond to the old man that very evening, two decades later, when a mild whistling was coming from the sakura in front of him.

His memories had awoken and demanded answers from him, especially in those places where he had remained silent...

And this was yet another occasion where he caught himself responding out loud to someone from the past. It was happening unexpectedly. His thoughts were winding and curling up like a snake in his head. It was only natural that they would shoot out like an arrow...

In the morning, he once again intentionally stared at the puddle. Beneath the frost, he noticed the soft smile of the daughter of winter, Yuki-onna... Suddenly, four or five dogs ran to the puddle, snarling at each other and beginning to break the layer of ice. Toshinari opened the window and exploded with anger. The dogs were startled and took up defensive poses, but seeing the safe distance between them, they continued to hit at the ice and gulp the water down to quench their thirst.

Disappointed by his helplessness, he turned away from the scene, and the tears began to flow as if the woman he loved was being raped before his very eyes while he could do nothing to prevent it...

He opened the book and, looking at a picture of an engraving of Yuki-onna by an eyewitness, he made the following note in his diary:

"I will never imagine her in a traditional kimono. Her soul seems to be escaping her somehow. Her body is squeezing her like a straitjacket... No, it is suppressing her marvel and weakening it... Clothes do not suit her. Perhaps they become a spiritual component of her, but at least a bit of her body must remain bare and breathe."

Perhaps Yuki-onna and I are fated to find each other in the world of words, but the tranquility of my solitude must not be disturbed, thought Toshinari.

***

Toshinari woke up from a dream, or rather, he jumped up at one point in the night and it was as if his waking surprised someone else who had wanted to escape the room. His heart was filled with the feeling that the stranger continued to be present in one of the dark corners of the room. He slowly got up from the bed and tried to get to the window as noiselessly as possible. The flooring creaked under his feet. He shut the window and moved aside. Then he crossed a dark corner of the room again and heard the floorboards creaking before silence descended again. That night, he understood that there are dreams that can break through from the other side and waking up suddenly can startle the newcomers; you have to either fall asleep again – as many people do – to allow the ghosts to slide back into your dream or you have to overcome your drowsiness and open a window so that the outsiders can leave and dissolve into the darkness…

"Never turn on the lamp. Never! Perhaps what you see will kill you. It could kill you!"

This was the advice left by those that had documented their encounters with Yuki-onna.

Instead of allowing any exits – in contrast to the advice he had received – he had closed the window and not gone back to sleep.

The mysterious dream gave him no peace. It returned during the day and ate away at his disposition. He tried to recall all the details of the dream with every ounce of muscle, flesh, and blood...

But the only thing left was a sensation that filled his heart with panic, a question that was constantly building up in his mind and consuming the oxygen around him – who had placed the words 'sun,' 'cherry tree,' and 'woman' on his table?

This question was driving him to insanity. Despite himself, he was expecting her around him. He could feel her leaning on his shoulder when he was by the window, sensing her weight and breathing. If he was standing, then she was sitting in the only chair by the desk or she was lying in the bed. *So it must be the items in the room that are giving birth to her,* thought Toshinari. *If I manage to achieve a state of total emptiness, she will vanish.*

He switched on the light, sat at the table, opened his diary, and wrote.

"I'm waking up of thirst recently, but I'm unable to move my hands because they are numb. When I'm asleep, my hands move to the top of my head and their blood starts to trickle down – they want to dry up. They are perhaps the only limbs in my body that are trying to commit suicide, and it seems like the others will follow if they succeed, and my organs drenched in their moribund desire will leap into my waking brain..."

He pressed the end of his pen hard into the last bit of this symbol. This poked a hole in the paper and the ink flowed across the white surface. He was going to extract and preserve only three words from this whole diary and it was even possible that those words were not present here. They might appear suddenly one day when he stared out the window.

Nevertheless, he would destroy his diary before writing that trinity of words. Hikikomoris should not leave behind any memoirs.

A real hermit would only search for new meaning in old memories. He would never allow the birth of new experiences, but with Yuki-onna…

***

An unexpected discovery occurred – the momentary recollection of the dream. Like a Bugaku performance, with the most detailed of slowness he was staring at the subject of his dream, which had appeared and stood in the room, with just the facial features obscured.

She ran along the seashore beneath the gulls, her head to the sky and her arms held out. She was imitating the birds and, ignoring the hard surface beneath her feet, she had almost achieved perfection with her flight. Her hair was flying in the direction of her raised heel – opening, waving in the air, and then returning in a jumble across her neck and face as if an artist had rushed to paint her escape to the edge of the canvas from where she was going to perform her final leap and never touch the ground again.

Toshinari bent down and touched her footprint, placing his palm in the indentation which was slowly being filled with water and, a short while later, the wave came and flooded him, but he kept holding on tightly to her trace, trying to keep it from vanishing…

She gathered her waves with restraint, like the sea, from Toshinari's shores, memories, mental images, and the locations where the two of them had been. She removed herself bit by bit from Toshinari's inner world…

Toshinari turned his gaze to the window where a fly was buzzing as it banged against the glass. 'I will let it free so that it can tell THEM that I am alive and that they should not waste time waiting for those three words.' He got up, went and opened the window, and then returned to his desk. A cold March wind filled the room and a fine and pleasant chill rushed over his body.

"I am an individual," he wrote in the diary and, as if getting a load off his chest, he thought, 'At least I have conducted a search…' This thought consoled him and the feeling that he had been the only one entered his lungs like a breath of air and warmed his belly. Finally, he gathered the courage to turn towards the door, where Setsuko was standing naked and shyly, and whispered:

"You should not leave. I will no longer try to discover everything about you…"

The naked woman's body (especially clenched) was like his soul. Setsuko's nudity was fragile.

The 女 symbol waved its tale at the edge of the abyss and slid into the darkness.

Toshinari fell asleep.

***

94

Tradition holds that if *Yuki-onna* appears to a hermit, that person will be visited a short while later by an indescribably beautiful woman who would become the hermit's wife. She would take care of her husband and raise their children. If the husband intentionally or accidently invaded the depths of his wife's soul and, asking questions of her past, discovered that the woman was the very same *Yuki-onna*, she would be forced to leave the man forever...

Notes

Hikikomori are people that have rejected a social life and, for various reasons, seek extreme isolation and confinement. There are such people in the USA as well where they are called 'basement dwellers' and in Europe, particularly in the United Kingdom, where they are called the nini generation (*NEET*).

Hanami (Jap. 花見, 'flower viewing') is the Japanese traditional custom of enjoying the transient beauty of flowers.

Ikebana is the Japanese art of flower arrangement. Every Japanese woman has certain skills in this form of art.

Yuki-onna is a supernatural female figure in Japanese legend, presented in ancient times as a witch or she-demon but also often as a beautiful bride and so on. She is known for having thousands of names and appearances. There are many witness accounts of visions of her that have been preserved in Japanese mythology as well as in personal memoirs.

Bugaku is a traditional Japanese form of theatrical art.